...ly Love You

A long, long time ago,
dinosaurs lived all over the world.

Those who lived in the north were very
different from those who lived in the south.
They had different shapes and colors.

They even spoke different languages.

TATSUYA MIYANISHI

MUSEYON, New York

One winter, snow started to fall in the valley where the Tyrannosaurus lived.

"Brrr . . ."
Shivering in the bitter cold, the Tyrannosaurus opened his eyes.
"So hungry . . . haven't eaten for days!"

A Tapejara, who had been curled up
on a rock, spoke to the Tyrannosaurus.

"Sir, beyond the mountains and far away,
there is a green forest where you will
find plenty of tasty food."
"Is that so? Then take me there!"
"Yes, sir! Follow me."

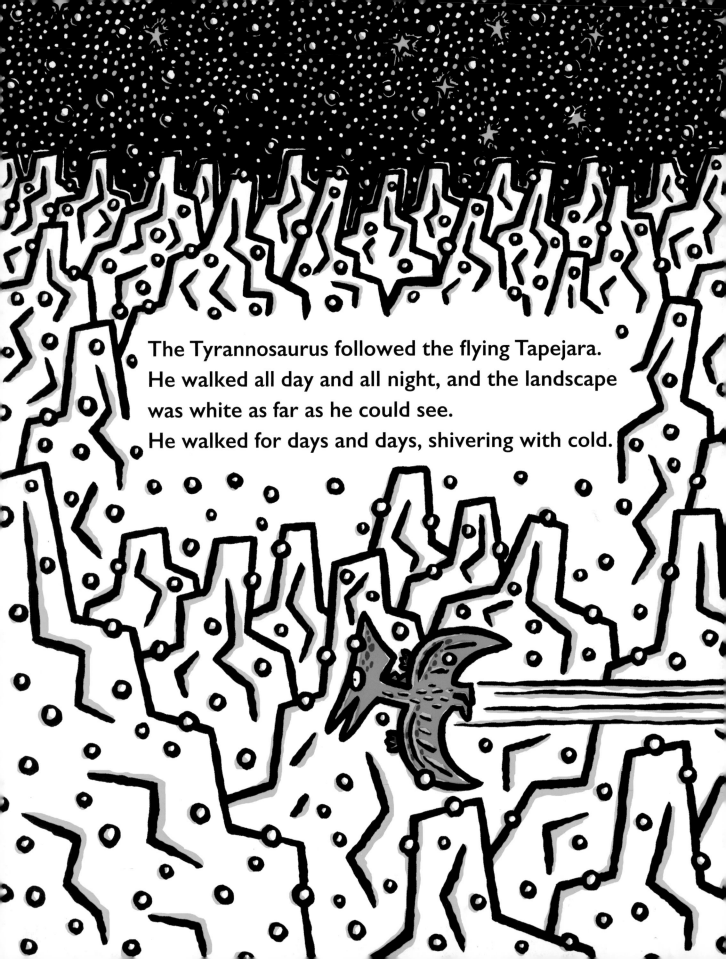

The Tyrannosaurus followed the flying Tapejara.
He walked all day and all night, and the landscape
was white as far as he could see.
He walked for days and days, shivering with cold.

He walked through mountains
and valleys. He was exhausted.
"H-hey, Tapejara, how much farther is it?"
"Just a little more, sir. Hold on, sir."
But the Tyrannosaurus mumbled.
"Oh no, I c-can't anymore. . . ."

BOOOM!

The Tyrannosaurus fell over.
The Tapejara flew down.
"Are you all right, sir? It's not that far to the green forest. I wish I could carry you on my back and take you there."

The Tapejara's words were kind, but there was

"D-d-don't mind me," murmured the Tyrannosaurus.
"You'd b-better go by yourself. I can't go any farther."
He closed his eyes.
"Wake up, please, Mr. Tyranno! Hang on, sir!"
No matter how many times the Tapejara called him,
the Tyrannosaurus did not answer.

The Tapejara's eyes glistened.
"Heh, heh, hehh . . . Are you dead now?"
the Tapejara asked.
Then . . .

CHOMP!

"Ouch! Tapejara, wh-what are you doing?"
The Tyrannosaurus opened his eyes.
"Heh, heh, heh . . . Oh! I guess you're not
dead yet. I lied about the green forest.
You are the tasty food I was talking
about!"

"You liar! You kept telling me good things.
You kept giving me sweet words.
What you did was unforgivable!"
With the last of his strength . . .

the Tyrannosaurus stood up and swung his tail.

THWACK!

The Tapejara flew away like
a leaf—TWIRL, TWIRL, TWIRL—and
disappeared back over the mountains.

Just then, in the distance the
Tyrannosaurus saw . . .
"It's the g-green forest!"
He walked toward it on shaky feet.

He heard small voices coming from the forest. *Food*, he thought. The Tyrannosaurus staggered into the forest. When he looked into the bushes . . .

there were three Homalocephales eating red berries.
Heh, heh, heh . . . I'm going to eat you!
"MUNCH, MUNCH!" the Tyrannosaurus said, drooling.

But the three small dinosaurs did not run away when
they saw him. Instead,
"MUNCH, MUNCH!"
"MUNCH, MUNCH!"
"MUNCH, MUNCH!"
they repeated with
big smiles.

Heh, heh, heh . . .
"Let's be friends,"
said the Tyrannosaurus.
"Now come to me!"
He picked the three up
and popped them into his mouth.
But . . .

the three Homalocephales clapped their hands happily in the Tyrannosaurus's mouth. He couldn't chew or swallow.

"MUNCH, MUNCH!"

"MUNCH, MUNCH!"

"MUNCH, MUNCH!

In their language, "munch, munch" meant "friend," but the Tyrannosaurus did not know that.

Ugh, I can't stand it! he thought.

MUNCH, MUNCH!

The three Homalocephales jumped around
happily inside the Tyrannosaurus's mouth.
He was so uncomfortable and hungry,
he thought he was going to faint. Then . . .

BOOM!

the Tyrannosaurus fell over.
The three small dinosaurs came out of his mouth,
surprised. They asked questions in their own language.
"DENEPPAH TAHW?"
"KO UOY ERA?"
"NIAP EVAH UOY?"

They looked worried as they talked, but the
Tyrannosaurus did not understand anything they said.
"I need to eat," he moaned. "P-please feed me. . . ."

"FEED ME?"

"YAS EH DID TAHW?"

"DNATSREDNU T'NOD."

The Tyrannosaurus thought,
They don't understand my language.

Just then, his stomach made a growling sound.
The three Homalocephales started
talking to each other again.

"YRGNUH SI EH!"

"DOOF EMOS DNIF S'TEL!"

"YRRUH!"

Then they ran away quickly.

A short time later,
the three came back,
their arms full of fish, clams,
and red berries.

"Yum, yum!"
The Tyrannosaurus gobbled the fish and clams,
but he didn't eat the berries.
"YUM, YUM!"
Two of the Homalocephale happily imitated him.

But the Tyrannosaurus realized that he had hurt the
feelings of the Homalocephale who had brought
the red berries. He felt sad and . . .

he took the berries, thinking,
These are not my favorite, but. . . .
He popped them into his mouth.
Yuck. . . . Oh, wait! "Yummy! Yummy! Yummy!"

Hearing the Tyrannosaurus, the three small
dinosaurs clapped their hands happily.
"YUMMY! YUMMY! YUMMY!"

They are happy for me, the Tyrannosaurus thought.
He was deeply touched by their kind hearts.
From that day on, the three Homalocephales
called the Tyrannosaurus
MUNCH, MUNCH.

As for the Tyrannosaurus, he called the one who brought him the fish **Ya**, the one who brought him the clams **Me**, and the one who brought him the red berries **Eee**.

Day after day,
Ya, **Me**, and **Eee** would gather fish, clams,
and red berries for the Tyrannosaurus.
Thanks to them,
he quickly recovered his strength.

Then one day,
Ya and **Me** started fighting over whether **Ya**'s
fish or **Me**'s clams should be given
to the Tyrannosaurus first.

RoAAAAARRR!

The Tyrannosaurus got angry.

Even though **Ya** and **Me** didn't understand his language, they were stunned.

Looking at them, the Tyrannosaurus smiled and said, "We are all friends here."

Ya, **Me**, and **Eee** also laughed and clapped their hands.

clap, clap, clap

That night, snuggling tightly against
the Tyrannosaurus, the three slept soundly.
In the middle of the night,
the Tyrannosaurus awoke and looked at them.
They look yummy, he thought, and his mouth watered.

But just then, **Eee** started to shake and hugged the
Tyrannosaurus tightly.

After that, the Tyrannosaurus wanted to know
more about his three small friends and tried to
teach them how to speak his language.

"**Ya**, can you say, 'I am **Ya**'?"
Ya listened and said, "Hammy **Ya**."
"No, not hammy. I am. Say, 'I am'!"
But **Ya** couldn't say it right.

"You're next, **Me**.
Say, 'Clams are yummy.'"
Then **Me** repeated,
"Yams are clummy."

Shaking his head, the Tyrannosaurus continued,
"**Eee**, you're next. Say, 'Let's be friends.'"
"Let's free bends."
"No! I said, 'Let's be friends.'"
"Bret's fee lends."
"No, no. Say, 'Let's . . . be . . . friends.'"
"Let's be fr-friends."

After all that, the only words that the three small dinosaurs could remember were "Yummy, yummy, yummy", "MUNCH, MUNCH," and "Let's be friends."

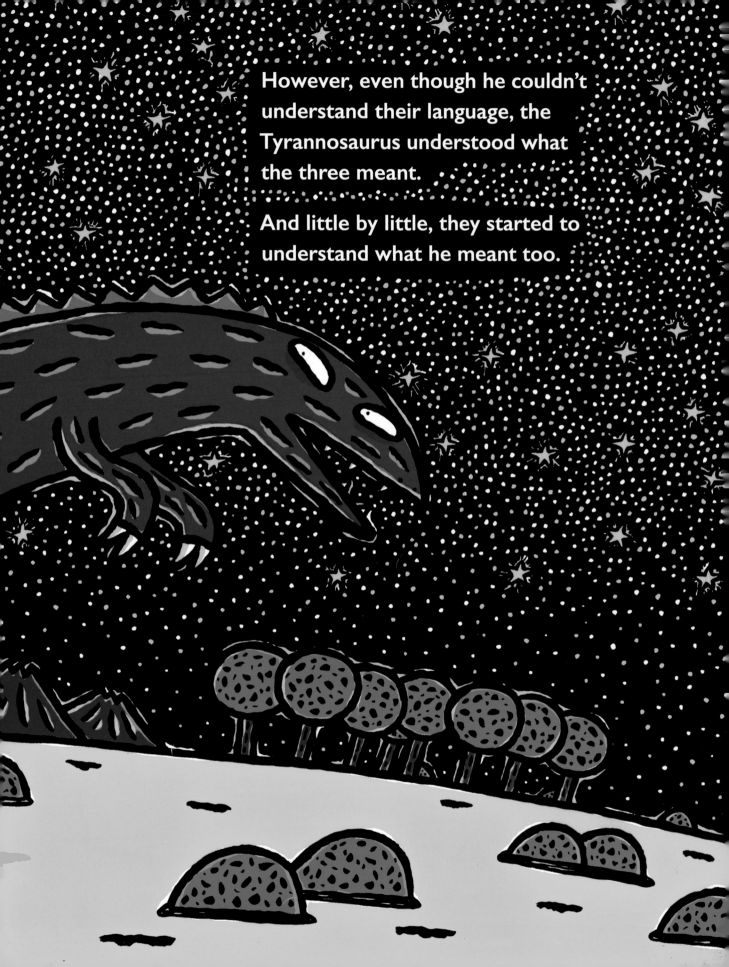

However, even though he couldn't understand their language, the Tyrannosaurus understood what the three meant.

And little by little, they started to understand what he meant too.

The Tyrannosaurus enjoyed being with **Ya**, **Me**, and **Eee**, and felt happy and comfortable with them.

He realized that while he had understood the words the Tapejara used, he never really felt comfortable with him.

And although he didn't understand the words the Homalocephales used, it didn't matter. They spoke the same language of the heart, and they understood each other.

One day, **Ya**, **Me**, and **Eee** sneaked out to gather red berries without telling the Tyrannosaurus.

Ya thought, *We're going to surprise MUNCH, MUNCH with lots of berries.*
Me thought, *I hope MUNCH, MUNCH is going to eat a lot.*
Eee thought, *I'll be so happy if MUNCH, MUNCH says, "Yummy! Yummy! Yummy!"*

Ya, **Me**, and **Eee** climbed a tree that had lots of red berries. Because they were not good at climbing trees, they fell out of the tree again and again.

They got many cuts and bruises. But they wanted to gather lots of berries for their friend.

Suddenly an Albertosaurus appeared.
"Heh, heh, heh . . . I'm going to eat you up!
MUNCH, MUNCH."

The Albertosaurus looked a lot like the Tyrannosaurus.
The three thought, *Since he speaks like MUNCH,
MUNCH, he could be our friend too.*

"MUNCH, MUNCH! Let's be friends,"
Eee said as he offered his red
berries to the Albertosaurus.

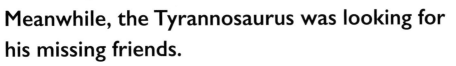

Meanwhile, the Tyrannosaurus was looking for
his missing friends.
Where have they gone? What if that Tapejara . . . ,
he thought.

"ROARR!"

The Albertosaurus's roar echoed from the red-berry forest.

The Tyrannosaurus ran as fast as he could.
He ran with all his strength.
And he reached the
woods . . .

just as the Albertosaurus was about
to gobble the three small dinosaurs.
"Leave those little ones alone!"
the Tyrannosaurus yelled.

He bit down on the Albertosaurus.

"WAAA!" the Albertosaurus yelled, and the three
Homalocephales jumped out of his mouth.
"What did I do? They came to me, saying, 'MUNCH,
MUNCH! Let's be friends.' So I mun—"

CHoMP!

"Never come to this
forest again!" the furious
Tyrannosaurus roared.
The Albertosaurus ran
away as fast as he could.

The Tyrannosaurus picked up the injured **Ya**, **Me**, and **Eee** from the ground and held them to his chest.

"I wish I had never taught you my language," he said. "You made me realize that even if we don't speak the same language, we can communicate with our hearts, and that's so much better. Thank you."

Snowflakes started falling in the forest.

The three were still holding the red berries firmly in their arms. The Tyrannosaurus took one red berry from each of them and put the berries in his mouth, tears running down his face. "You did this for me. Thank you. I promise I'll take care of you until you're better."

"Friends with MUNCH, MUNCH," **Ya** said, and softly closed his eyes.
"MUNCH, MUNCH yummy," **Me** said, and gently closed his eyes.
"These taste so good," said the Tyrannosaurus.
"Yummy! Yummy! Yummy !"
Hearing that, **Eee** smiled and said,

"UOY EVOL YLLAER I."

Then **Eee** slowly closed his eyes.

The Tyrannosaurus did not understand **Eee**'s words, but somehow he knew that **Eee** had said,

"I REALLY LOVE YOU."

The Tyrannosaurus curled himself around his three small friends as the pure white snow fell softly around them all.

About Author

Born in 1956, **Tatsuya Miyanishi** is one of the most popular children's book creators in Japan. His Tyrannosaurus series has sold more than three million copies and has been translated into many languages. Miyanishi has won the Kodansha Cultural Award for Picture Books, as well as the Kenbuchi Picture Book Grand Prize.

I REALLY LOVE YOU

Watashi wa Anata wo Aishiteimasu © 2007 Tatsuya Miyanishi
All rights reserved.

Names: Miyanishi, Tatsuya, 1956- author, illustrator. | Gharbi, Mariko Shii, translator. | Kaplan, Simone, editor.
Title: I really love you / Tatsuya Miyanishi ; Mariko Shii Gharbi, translator ; Simone Kaplan, editor.
Other titles: Watashi wa anata wo aishiteimasu. English
Description: New York : Museyon, [2019] | Series: Tyrannosaurus series ; book 6. | "Originally published in Japan in 2007 by POPLAR Publishing Co., Ltd."--Title page verso. |
Identifiers: ISBN: 9781940842264 | LCCN: 2018965697
Subjects: LCSH: Tyrannosaurus rex--Juvenile fiction. | Pachycephalosauridae--Juvenile fiction. | Albertosaurus--Juvenile fiction. | Dinosaurs--Juvenile fiction. | Love--Juvenile fiction. | Friendship--Juvenile fiction. | Intercultural communication--Juvenile fiction. | Interpersonal communication--Juvenile fiction. | CYAC: Tyrannosaurus rex--Fiction. | Pachycephalosauridae--Fiction. | Albertosaurus--Fiction. | Dinosaurs--Fiction. | Love--Fiction. | Friendship--Fiction. | Communication--Fiction. | Interpersonal communication--Fiction. | BISAC: JUVENILE FICTION / Animals / Dinosaurs & Prehistoric Creatures.
Classification: LCC: PZ7.M699575 I185 2019 | DDC: [E]--dc23

Published in the United States and Canada by:
Museyon Inc.
333 East 45th Street
New York, NY 10017

Museyon is a registered trademark.
Visit us online at www.museyon.com

Originally published in Japan in 2007 by POPLAR Publishing Co., Ltd.
English translation rights arranged with POPLAR Publishing Co., Ltd.

Printed in China

ISBN 9781940842264